A NOTE TO PARENTS

Reading Aloud with Your Child

Research shows that reading books aloud is the single most valuable support parents can provide in helping children learn to read.

- Be a ham! The more enthusiasm you display, the more your child will enjoy the book.
- Run your finger underneath the words as you read to signal that the print carries the story.
- Leave time for examining the illustrations more closely; encourage your child to find things in the pictures.
- Invite your youngster to join in whenever there's a repeated phrase in the text.
- Link up events in the book with similar events in your child's life.
- If your child asks a question, stop and answer it. The book can be a means to learning more about your child's thoughts.

Listening to Your Child Read Aloud

The support of your attention and praise is absolutely crucial to your child's continuing efforts to learn to read.

- If your child is learning to read and asks for a word, give it immediately so that the meaning of the story is not interrupted. DO NOT ask your child to sound out the word.
- On the other hand, if your child initiates the act of sounding out, don't intervene.
- If your child is reading along and makes what is called a miscue, listen for the sense of the miscue. If the word "road" is substituted for the word "street," for instance, no meaning is lost. Don't stop the reading for a correction.
- If the miscue makes no sense (for example, "horse" for "house"), ask your child to reread the sentence because you're not sure you understand what's just been read.
- Above all else, enjoy your child's growing command of print and make sure you give lots of praise. *You are your child's first teacher—and the most important one. Praise from you is critical for further risk-taking and learning.*

—Priscilla Lynch
Ph.D., New York University
Educational Consultant

Dedicated to all the great kids
who played on my soccer teams.
— CM

To Martha and Emily,
my favorite little kickers
— JR

Claudio Marzollo was a children's soccer coach for eight years. He lives with his wife, Jean, a children's book author, in Cold Spring, N.Y.

LIBRARY OF CONGRESS CATALOGING-IN-PUBLICATION DATA
Marzollo, Claudio.
      Kenny and the little kickers / by Claudio Marzollo : illustrated by Jackie Rogers.
        p. cm. — (Hello reader)
      "Level 2"
      Summary: Although he feels shy and out of place on the playing field, Kenny agrees to try soccer.
      ISBN: 0-590-45417-X
      [1. Soccer — Fiction.] I. Rogers, Jacqueline. ill. II. Title.
   III. Series.
   PZ7.M36875Ke 1992
   [E] — dc20   91-16707
                                                                  CIP
                                                                   AC

Text copyright © 1992 by Claudio Marzollo.
Illustrations copyright © 1992 by Jacqueline Rogers.
All rights reserved. Published by Scholastic Inc.
CARTWHEEL BOOKS is a trademark of Scholastic Inc.
HELLO READER! is a registered trademark of Scholastic Inc.

12 11 10 9 8 7 6 5   4 5 6 7/9

Printed in the U.S.A.   23

First Scholastic printing, May 1992

Kenny and the Little Kickers

by Claudio Marzollo • Illustrated by Jacqueline Rogers

Hello Reader! — Level 2

Scholastic Inc.
Cartwheel B·O·O·K·S™

New York   Toronto   London   Auckland   Sydney

"Soccer starts today!"
said Kenny's dad.

"Do you want to join
the Little Kickers?"
Kenny said no.
He felt too big and fat
to play soccer.

Kenny's dad said,
"Let's go see."
They drove to the field.
Kids were getting T-shirts,
red ones and green ones.

One green one was left.
"Do you want it?" asked the coach.
Kenny said no.
"Come on," said his dad.
"Come on," said the kids.
"Come on," said the coach.

So Kenny put on the green T-shirt.

Everyone ran down the field.
Kenny was last.

Everyone ran back.
Kenny was last again.

They kicked the ball
between two cones.
Kenny missed.

The Green team passed
the ball back and forth.
Kenny kicked the ball
to a Red player by mistake.

Kenny went over to his dad.
"Can we please
go home now?" he asked.
"Try a little longer,"
said his dad.
"It's almost over."

"Let's try a little game,"
said the coach.
"Red shirts go here.
Green shirts go there."
The coach looked at Kenny.

"You look like a strong kicker,"
he said.
"Do you want to be a fullback?"
Kenny wanted to say no,
but he didn't say anything.

"Kenny," said the coach.
"Your job is to keep
the Reds from kicking
the ball into the Green net.
Whenever the ball comes your way,
kick it down the field
as far as you can. Okay?"
Kenny wanted to say no,
but he didn't.

Kenny stood on the field.
Red kids were coming his way.
They were very fast.

Kenny wished
he were back home
watching cartoons.
A Red player
kicked the ball
right toward him!
Yikes!
What was he going to do?

"Kick it!" yelled his father.
"Kick it!" yelled the Greens.
"Kick it!" yelled the coach.
The ball rolled up to Kenny
and stopped.
It was sitting right
in front of him.
Should he kick it?

No, no, no, YES!
Kenny kicked the ball
as hard as he could.

It flew over the Greens.
It flew over the Reds.
It flew all the way
to the Red goal
and went in!

"A goal!" shouted the coach.
"Way to go!" yelled Kenny's dad.
"Hooray for Kenny!"
yelled the Greens.

From that day on,
every Saturday
Kenny played soccer
and loved it.